To Saffy – for making me smile
when nothing else could.
– I.D.

For Ollie, my support dog and
Steve, my support human.
– S.C.

First published 2021

EK Books
an imprint of Exisle Publishing Pty Ltd
PO Box 864, Chatswood, NSW 2057, Australia
226 High Street, Dunedin, 9016, New Zealand
www.ekbooks.org

A CiP record for this book is available from the National Library of Australia.

ISBN 978-1-925820-95-9

Designed by Mark Thacker
Typeset in Minya Nouvelle 18 on 26pt
Printed in China

This book uses paper sourced under ISO 14001 guidelines from well-
managed forests and other controlled sources.

10 9 8 7 6 5 4 3 2 1

COOKIE

ISABELLE DUFF AND SUSANNAH CRISPE

I don't remember much before Girl.
I was in a very shaky box for a long time.
A time even longer than my tongue.

When the very shaky box stopped shaking,
there was Girl.

Girl was warm and good to lick ... And she had ball.

Girl said I was Cookie, because cookies make things better.

'I love you, Cookie,' she said.

We went to find a boy that first day. 'Our boy,' Girl said.

The boy was called Stopit, but sometimes
Girl called him Shoosh instead.

He called her You're-not-the-boss-of-me.

Together we found the yummiest smells.
I had a lead so Girl didn't get lost.

When it was dark, Girl tucked me into
a cuddle. Then she got in her big cuddle,
and we went to sleep.

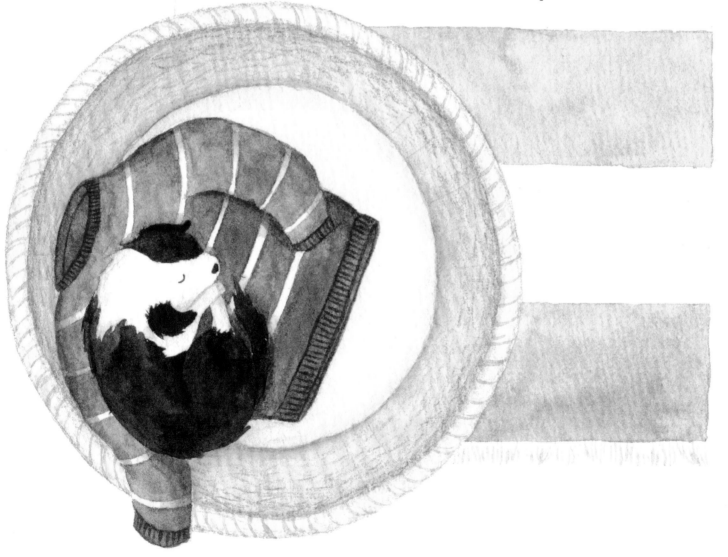

The next day, Girl was sad.
She didn't want to play.

Stopit was there. He played with me,
but I wanted to play with Girl.

So I took her a present.

'I love you, my Cookie,' she said.

Girl tried to play.
But she was too sad.
So we cuddled instead.

Playing is better than cuddles,
but Girl is very good at cuddles,
especially when she's sad.

Girl's sad made Mama sad too.
I was good at sad.
You can lick it off, you know.

'I love you the most, my Cookie,' Girl said.

We went for lots of walks
and smelled lots of smelly smells ...

and made lots of friends.

But mostly we did
lots of chewing.

'I love you,
silly Cookie,' said Girl.

Girl still slept in her big cuddle a lot.
Maybe it wasn't working, I thought.

So I tried to share mine.

'I love you, little Cookie,' Girl said.

I got so big I could take Girl on adventures.
She taught me good games, like how to sit,
and stop, and come.

Those games have cheese.
I like cheese.

Sometimes nothing could make Girl smile.
Except me.
Because I do such good bounces.

'I love you, gorgeous Cookie,'
said Girl.

We played. We cuddled. We chewed. We ate.
And when Girl got sad
I licked her happy again.

We rolled and smelled and
ran and chewed some more.
And there was less sad
on Girl to lick.

But she tasted nice so
I licked her anyway.

'I love you, my crazy Cookie,'
Girl said.

I got so big I could run as fast as Stopit.

And help Dad when he got stuck.

I helped so much Girl got happier.
And everyone is happier when Girl is happier.

Especially me.

Now we leap and we zoom
and we chase and we hug.

But most of all, I lick my Girl.

'I love you, my Cookie,' says Girl.

I love you too, my Girl.